THE URBANA FREE LIBRARY

3 1230 00864 4516

W9-AHQ-901

DISCARDED BY THE
URBANA FREE LIBRARY

The Urbana Free Library

To renew: call 217-367-4057
or go to "*urbanafreelibrary.org*"
and select "Renew/Request Items"

With

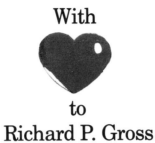

to
Richard P. Gross

Copyright © 1987 by Ruth Heller
All rights reserved. This book, or parts thereof, may not be
reproduced in any form without permission in writing from the publisher.
A PaperStar Book, published in 1998 by The Putnam & Grosset Group,
345 Hudson Street, New York, NY 10014.
PaperStar is a registered trademark of The Putnam Berkley Group, Inc.
The PaperStar logo is a trademark of The Putnam Berkley Group, Inc.
Originally published in 1987 by Grosset & Dunlap.
Published simultaneously in Canada
Manufactured in China
Library of Congress Catalog Card Number: 87-80254
ISBN 978-0-698-11354-1

22 23 24 25 26 27 28 29 30

RUTH HELLER

WORLD OF LANGUAGE

A CACHE OF JEWELS

and Other Collective Nouns

Written and illustrated by
RUTH HELLER

PAPERSTAR

Penguin Young Readers Group

A word that means a collection of things,
like a

CACHE

of jewels
for the crowns of kings…

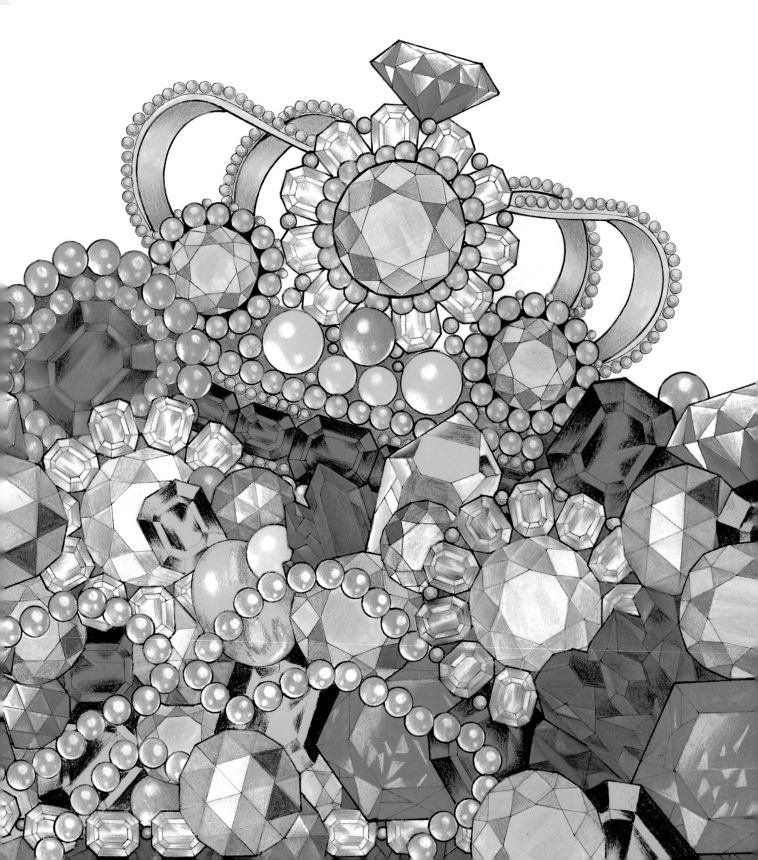

or a **BATCH** of bread all warm and brown,

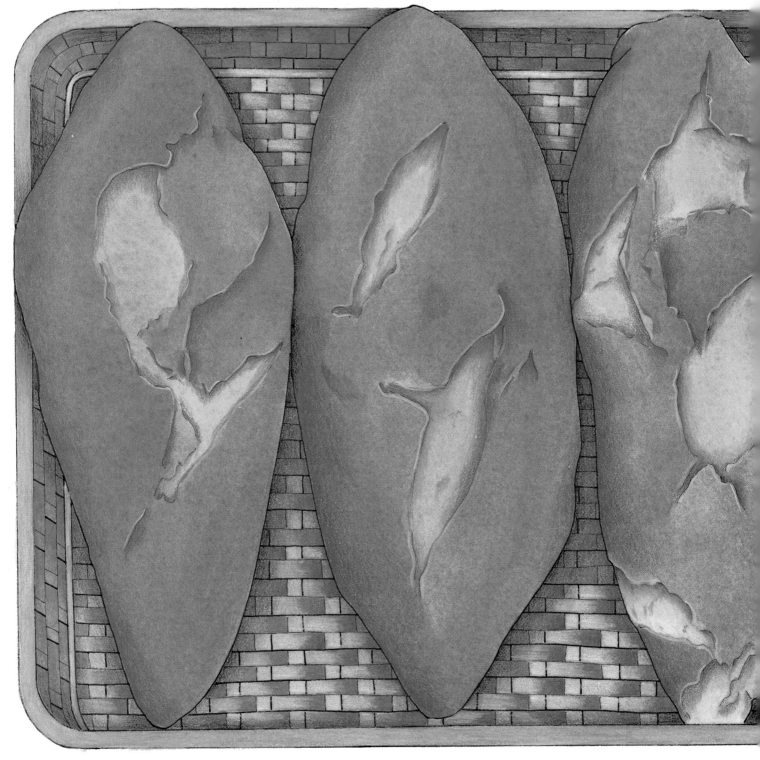

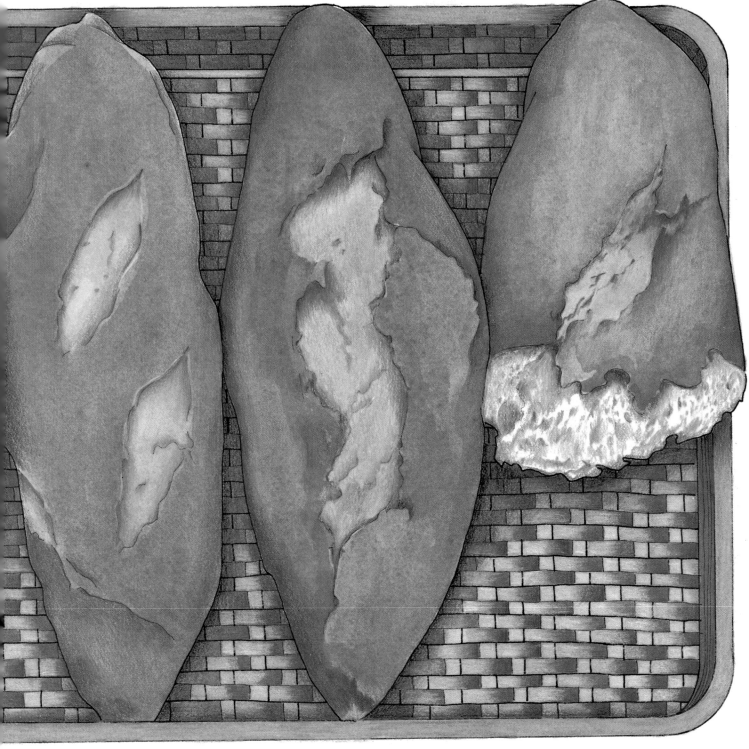

a SCHOOL of fish

a **GAM** of whales

a **FLEET** of ships
with
purple sails

a BUNCH of bananas

a
CLUSTER
of
grapes

a
BEVY
of
beauties
.

all different
shapes

a **MUSTER** of peacocks

a
FLOCK
of
sheep

a
HOST
of
angels
fast
asleep

a BOUQUET
of flowers

a
SWARM
of
bees

a **KINDLE** of kittens
a
POD of peas

a **PARCEL** of
penguins

a
FOREST
of
trees

a
COVEN
of
witches
as
scary
as
these

a **DRIFT** of swans

a **CLUMP**
of reeds

a
BED
of
oysters

a
STRING
of
beads

a
BROOD
of
chicks

a
CLUTCH
of
eggs

a
LITTER
of puppies on wobbly legs

a
PRIDE
of lions

a **LOCK** of hair

an
ARMY
of ants
from
here to…

there....

About five hundred years ago
knights and ladies in the know
used only very special words
to describe their flocks or herds.

These words are used by us today,
but some were lost along the way,
and new ones have been added too.

I've included quite a few.

And there are more of these group terms
like sleuth of bears
or clew of worms
or rafter of turkeys
walk of snails
leap of leopards
covey of quails.

But nouns aren't all collective,
and if I'm to be effective,
I'll tell about the other nouns
and adjectives and verbs.

All of them are parts of speech.

What fun!
I'll write a book for each.

—*Ruth Heller*

<u>Note:</u> One collective noun can describe many groups, as in a **host** of angels, daffodils, monks, thoughts, or sparrows.

One group can be described by more than one collective noun as in a **gam** of whales, a **mob** of whales, a **pod** of whales, a **school** of whales, or a **run** of whales.

1479011